MORE
MARY-MARY

Written and Illustrated by

JOAN G. ROBINSON

D1437817

COLLINS : LIONS

First published 1958 by George C. Harrap & Co Ltd
First published in Lions 1972
by William Collins Sons and Co Ltd
14 St James's Place, London sw1
Second Impression June 1974

© Joan G. Robinson 1958

Printed in Great Britain
by William Collins Sons and Co Ltd, Glasgow

CONDITIONS OF SALE:
This book is sold subject to the condition
that it shall not by way of trade or otherwise,
be lent, re-sold, hired out or otherwise circulated
without the publisher's prior consent in any form of
binding or cover other than that in which it is
published and without a similar condition
including this condition being imposed
on the subsequent purchaser

Contents

For
Sylvia May

ONE

Mary-Mary has a Photograph taken

One day Mary-Mary's mother said, 'I think it is time you had your photographs taken again. We haven't had a proper one done since you were all quite little.'

'Mary-Mary is still quite little,' said Miriam.

'But she was a baby last time,' said Martyn.

'And she kept wriggling and screeching,' said Mervyn.

'And pulling my hair-ribbon,' said Meg.

Then they all started talking at once, saying, 'Don't let's have our photographs taken all to-

" she was a baby last time."

gether.' 'Let's each have one of our own.' 'Then they can all go in separate frames.'

But Mother said, 'I'm afraid that would cost far too much. Besides, I should like to have one of all five of you. Then I could put it on top of my writing-desk, where all my friends could see it.'

'What shall we wear?' said Miriam.

'Jeans and a jersey,' said Martyn.

'Space suits,' said Mervyn.

'My party dress,' said Meg.

'I shan't wear anything,' said Mary-Mary.

'*What!*' said all the others.

'Anything special, I mean,' said Mary-Mary.

Mother said she didn't think it mattered much what they wore so long as they were all clean and tidy, and remembered to smile and look pleasant.

'You will have to sit quite still, Mary-Mary,' said Miriam.

'And not make silly faces,' said Martyn.

'Or talk all the time,' said Mervyn.

'And you have to smile at the camera,' said Meg.

'I think it's silly to smile at a camera,' said Mary-Mary. '*I* shall smile at the man. Unless I don't like him. Then I shan't smile at all.'

'It might be a lady,' said Meg.

'I still shan't smile if I don't like her,' said Mary-Mary.

Then Miriam, Martyn, Mervyn, and Meg all started saying together, 'Mother, Mary-Mary's going to spoil the photograph.' 'She says she's not going to smile.' 'Don't let's have it done with her.' 'Can't she have a snapshot taken in the garden?'

But Mother said, 'Don't be silly, all of you. Of course Mary-Mary will smile. Just leave her alone and I'm sure she'll behave beautifully.'

Mary-Mary had just begun planning what awful face she would make in front of the camera, because the others were all so sure she was going to spoil the photograph. But when she heard Mother say she was sure she would behave beautifully she changed her mind.

She began practising her smile instead. She smiled at the floor and she smiled at the ceiling. She smiled at the table, she smiled at the chairs, she smiled at everything she could see. But the more she smiled the queerer it felt, and after a while she didn't feel as if she was smiling at all. It made her face ache. So, just to give her face a rest, she blew out her cheeks and crossed her eyes. Then she tried on the smile again.

'Why are you making such awful faces, Mary-Mary?' said Miriam.

— and she smiled at the ceiling —

'I'm not,' said Mary-Mary, rather surprised. 'I'm getting ready to have my photograph taken.'

'Oh, dear, I *know* she's going to spoil it!' said Miriam to Mother. '*Can't* we all be done separately?'

And Martyn and Mervyn said, 'Yes, do let's.'

And Meg said, 'Can I have mine in the silver frame?'

But Mother said, 'No. I think you're all being very silly. And, in any case, there's a photograph in the silver frame already—one of Miriam and Martyn when they were babies. Now, do leave Mary-Mary alone. She'll be perfectly all right if you don't worry her.'

Mary-Mary went out and looked in the hall mirror to see if her smile really looked as funny as it felt. She tried smiling at herself for quite a long time. But the longer she looked at her face in the glass the queerer it looked.

'It's funny,' she said to herself. 'It's quite easy to smile by mistake, but it's really very difficult to smile on purpose. Perhaps it's because I'm not smiling *at* anyone. I'll try again at dinner-time.'

Then, just to give her face a rest, she tried making some interesting new faces that were very ugly indeed.

'They may come in useful next time the others are rude to me,' she said to herself.

At dinner-time Miriam said to Mary-Mary, 'Why are you making that extraordinary face at me?'

'I'm not,' said Mary-Mary. 'I'm smiling at you.'

'Well, don't,' said Miriam. 'It looks awful.'

Mary-Mary made one of her interesting new faces instead, but Miriam pretended not to see.

A little later Mother said, 'What's the matter,

Mary-Mary, dear? Have you got a tummy ache?'

'No,' said Mary-Mary. 'I'm smiling at you.'

Mother looked surprised. Then she said, 'That isn't your ordinary smile, darling. What are you doing it for?'

'I'm practising for the photograph,' said Mary-Mary.

'There you are, you see!' said Miriam, Martyn, Mervyn, and Meg, all together. 'What did we tell you?' 'She is going to spoil it!' 'She's practising all these awful faces to make in front of the camera.'

Mary-Mary didn't make the rest of her interesting new faces at them, because no one was looking at her. Instead she decided to save them for another time, and went away to find Moppet, her toy mouse.

Moppet was lying under the chest of drawers in the bedroom. Mary-Mary pulled him out, brushed the fluff off his fur, and stared closely into his tiny black eyes.

'Watch carefully, Moppet,' she said. Then she smiled at him.

'What did I look like?' asked Mary-Mary.

'Oh, you looked just like a toothpaste lady!' she said in Moppet's voice.

'Good,' said Mary-Mary. 'I hoped I did.'

— tried making some interesting new faces —

She went back to the sitting-room, put her head round the door, and said, '*Moppet* says I smile just like a toothpaste lady.'

Then, before anyone could answer, she shut the door quickly and went away to play in the garden.

The very next day they all got ready to go to the photographer's. They had their shoes polished, their nails scrubbed, and their hair brushed, and Mother said she had never seen them all looking so clean and neat and tidy all at the same time.

When they got to the photographer's a lady with golden hair smiled at them a great deal, and showed them into a room behind the shop, where there was a thick carpet on the floor and a large camera standing in the corner.

Mary-Mary liked the colour of the lady's hair very much, but she decided to save her smile for when the photograph was taken, in case she couldn't do it twice.

The lady found a chair for Mother in a corner behind the camera; then she looked at all the children, still smiling, and said to Mother, 'How would you like them taken—all together or one at a time?'

Mother said, 'All together, please. I think I would like them standing in a row.'

'Yes,' said the lady, 'that would make a very nice picture.'

So Miriam, Martyn, Mervyn, Meg and Mary-Mary all stood in a row together, while the lady turned on a very bright light and did things to the camera. She kept smiling all the time as she bobbed up and down this way and that, looking at them from every direction and saying, 'Yes, that's lovely. Now keep just like that, can you?'

Then she went behind the camera.

Mary-Mary put on the smile she had been practising so as to be ready for the photograph to be taken. Then she looked out of the corner

"Now keep just like that, can you?"

of her eye to see if the others were smiling too. But Miriam, Martyn, Mervyn, and Meg were all looking at her.

Miriam had her eyes wide open and was shaking her head at her. Martyn was frowning. Mervyn had his mouth screwed up into a round 'O.' And Meg was looking very cross indeed.

Mary-Mary thought they looked so funny, all standing in a row making faces at her without saying a word, that she suddenly laughed out loud.

'All right,' said the lady, bobbing about be-

~ all standing in a row making faces at her ~

hind the camera. 'Now we'll try another one, shall we?'

Every one looked surprised. Then Mary-Mary said, 'Another what?'

'Another picture,' said the lady. 'I've taken one already, but I think some of you moved. Now, are you all ready?'

Mary-Mary began smiling again, so as to be ready for the next photograph to be taken.

'Tell her to stop making faces,' whispered Miriam to Martyn.

'Tell her to stop making faces,' whispered Martyn to Mervyn.

'Tell her to stop making faces,' whispered Mervyn to Meg.

'Tell her to stop making faces,' whispered Meg to Mary-Mary.

Mary-Mary looked at the lady and saw that she was looking at them all with her eyes screwed up and her head on one side.

She turned to Meg and whispered back, 'No. You tell her. I don't think she can help it.'

Then Miriam, Martyn, Mervyn, and Meg all whispered at once, 'No, *you*. Stop making faces.'

'Oh, I thought you meant the lady!' whispered Mary-Mary, and she burst out laughing again.

Then the lady said, 'Thank you very much. I think that will do nicely.'

After that they all put on their hats and coats, and Mother talked to the lady about when the photographs would be ready and where they were to be sent. Then they all set off home again.

On the way Miriam said to Mother, 'I'm sure Mary-Mary spoiled the photograph. She kept making faces and laughing.'

But Mother said, 'Oh, no, I'm sure it will be lovely. Wait till you see it. I expect we shall all be surprised how nice it is.'

A week later there was a loud *rat-tat* on the front door, and the postman handed in a large, stiff envelope, addressed to Mother.

'Oh, it's our photograph!' cried Miriam.

'Can we open it?' said Martyn.

'No, give it to Mother,' said Mervyn.

'Let's have a look,' said Meg.

'Me too,' said Mary-Mary.

And they all crowded round while Mother opened the envelope.

Then every one said, 'Oh!' in a very surprised voice, and Mother started laughing. But all the others just stared at the picture as if they couldn't believe their eyes.

For there, in a row, stood Miriam with her eyes wide open, Martyn frowning, Mervyn with his mouth screwed up into a round 'O,' and Meg looking very cross indeed. And they were all staring at Mary-Mary. But Mary-Mary herself, right at the end of the row, was looking just the way people ought to look in photographs, all smiling and jolly.

'Oh, but it's *awful*!' said Miriam.

'I look *terrible*,' said Martyn.

'Look at *me*, then,' said Mervyn.

'How *dreadful*!' said Meg.

Mother smiled at the photograph, holding it up in front of her.

'But it's lovely of Mary-Mary,' she said. 'It's quite the best photograph we've ever had of her. And I've always wanted a proper photograph to show to all my friends.'

Then Miriam, Martyn, Mervyn, and Meg all

said together, 'But you *can't* show people a photograph like that!' 'We look awful.' 'Every one will laugh at us.' 'It isn't fair.'

'No,' said Mother, 'I don't think I can. I shall have to cut Mary-Mary off the end, and have you four done again another day.'

So that is just what she did. She cut Mary-Mary, all smiling and jolly, off the end of the photograph and found that it just fitted the frame which had the picture of Miriam and Martyn, when they were babies, in it.

'I think we might put that old one in the photograph album now,' she said. And she took it out and slipped the new one of Mary-Mary into the frame instead. Then she hid the rest of the photograph in a drawer in the writing-desk, promising she wouldn't show it to anyone but Father. And she took Miriam, Martyn, Mervyn, and Meg to the photographer's again another day.

And after that, whenever Mother's friends came to visit her, they would see two photographs on top of the writing-desk. At one end a photograph of Miriam, Martyn, Mervyn, and Meg all in a row, smiling rather carefully, as if they were afraid of making funny faces; and at the other end, in a silver frame all to herself, a photograph of Mary-Mary looking just the way people ought to look in photographs, all smiling and jolly.

So Mary-Mary didn't spoil the photograph,
after all, and that is the end of the story.

TWO

Mary-Mary and the Snow Giant

One day Mary-Mary woke up and found that some more snow had fallen in the night. There had been snow for two or three days, but it had all got trampled and dirty. Now there was a new white covering over everything. It looked very pretty.

Mary-Mary decided to go out before breakfast and be the very first person to make foot prints in the new snow. She dressed quickly and quietly, put on her coat and crept downstairs. In the hall she found Father's boots.

'Just the thing,' said Mary-Mary to herself. 'I shall feel like a proper snow giant in those.' And she stepped inside them, shoes and all, and went quietly out into the back garden. And nobody else knew anything about it at all.

At breakfast-time Mary-Mary's big brothers and sisters were all very excited, talking about the new snow.

'Let's divide the lawn into four,' said Miriam; 'then we can each have our own part. I shall make a snow palace in mine.'

—and nobody else
   knew anything about it at all—

'Good idea,' said Martyn. 'I shall make a big white horse in mine.'

'I shall make an igloo and be an Eskimo,' said Mervyn.

'And I shall make a snow queen,' said Meg.

Mary-Mary said, 'I shall do something better than all of those. I shall make a snow giant.'

But Miriam said, 'No, we can't divide the lawn into five.'

And Martyn said, 'You messed it all up last time, making snowballs and things.'

And Mervyn said, 'You go round the edges or play in the front.'

And Meg said, 'Anyway, there isn't any such thing as a snow giant.'

'Oh, yes, there is!' said Mary-Mary.

'Oh, no, there isn't,' said all the others.

Mary-Mary looked at them all and said slowly, in her most important grown-up voice, 'There's been a snow giant in the garden already this morning.'

'Rubbish,' they said. 'We don't believe it.'

'Moppet knows there was a snow giant,' said Mary-Mary. 'Don't you, Moppet?' Then she squeaked, 'Yes,' in Moppet's voice.

But the others just said, 'Nonsense. Don't take any notice of her.' Then they all went off to put on their coats and Wellingtons, and go out in the garden.

Mary-Mary stayed in the kitchen with Mother and helped to put away the spoons and forks. In a minute Martyn came to the back door and said, 'Mother, has anyone been in our garden?'

'No,' said Mother, 'not this morning.'

'Not Father even?' said Martyn.

'No,' said Mother, 'not Father even. He went out early. No one else has been here.'

'Only the snow giant,' said Mary-Mary.

'Oh, don't be silly,' said Martyn, and went out again.

Mary-Mary could hear the others all whispering together outside the back door. 'It must

— putting their feet carefully into the big footprints —

have been a burglar!' 'Let's find out where he went!' 'Don't let Mary-Mary come—she'll spoil it.' 'We'll track him down.'

Then they all went creeping along to the garden again.

Mary-Mary stood on a chair and looked out of the kitchen window. She saw Miriam, Martyn, Mervyn, and Meg all walking in a line round the garden, putting their feet carefully into the big footprints she had left, one after the other, and she began laughing to herself because they looked as if they were playing Follow my Leader.

'Why don't you go out and play too?' said Mother.

So Mary-Mary went and put on her own coat and Wellingtons.

As she was going out the others all came along to the house again to find Mother. They stood in a row in the doorway, looking very solemn and mysterious.

Then Miriam said, 'Mother, we think we ought to tell you—there's been a strange man walking in our garden, and we think he may have been a burglar.'

'Good gracious!' said Mother. 'How do you know?'

'It wasn't a burglar,' said Mary-Mary. 'It was the—'

'Be quiet, Mary-Mary,' said the others.

'We tracked his footprints in the snow,' said Martyn.

'Dearie me!' said Mother. 'I wonder who it was.'

'It was the snow giant,' said Mary-Mary. 'Once upon a time there was a huge, great snow giant and he——'

'Oh, be quiet, Mary-Mary,' said all the others.

'He had huge great boots on,' said Miriam.

('That's what I was going to say,' said Mary-Mary.)

'He went into the shed,' said Martyn.

('Yes, so did the snow giant,' said Mary-Mary.)

'And came out again,' said Mervyn.

('So did the snow giant,' said Mary-Mary.)

'And walked all the way round the garden,' said Meg.

('So did the—')

'BE QUIET, Mary-Mary,' they all shouted.

'No,' said Mother, 'don't shout like that. If Mary-Mary wants to tell us something let her. What is it, Mary-Mary?'

'Well,' said Mary-Mary, 'once upon a time there was a huge, great snow giant –'

'There's no such thing,' said Miriam.

'– and he came in the garden early in the morning—'

'Not *our garden*,' said Martyn.

'—and he sat down in the middle of the lawn—'

'I don't believe it,' said Mervyn.

'—and had snow for breakfast and—'

'Rubbish,' said Meg.

'No, don't interrupt,' said Mother. 'Go on, Mary-Mary.'

But Mary-Mary was getting cross at being interrupted so much; so she finished off by saying very quickly and loudly, '—and then four silly great children who thought they knew everything came walking into the garden, and they were all rather cross and grumbly, and all their names began with an M. They were called Mumbling, Muttering, Moaning, and—and Mumps, and when the snow giant saw them all grumbling round the garden he—'

But the others all shouted, 'Be *quiet*, Mary-Mary! Why don't you go and play in the front garden and leave us alone?'

So Mary-Mary said, 'All right, I will. I thought you wanted to know, but if you don't want to know I won't tell you.' And she walked away with her nose in the air.

The snow in the front was nice and thick, and no one had trodden on it except down the path. Mary-Mary decided to make a real snow giant, just outside the sitting-room window.

'Then they'll *have* to believe in him,' she said, 'when they see him looking in at the window.'

She began making a big pile of snow under the window, and was still hard at work when the postman came in at the gate.

'Hallo,' he said. 'What are you making?'

Mary-Mary told him. 'Would you like to help?' she asked.

The postman said, no, he was sorry he

couldn't help because he'd got work to do. But, all the same, he stopped long enough to show her how to roll some really big snowballs and pile them, one on top of the other, under the window; and soon the snow giant was as high as the window-sill.

'I must be off now,' said the postman; 'but that's quite a nice start for a snowman.'

'Thank you very much,' said Mary-Mary. 'You *have* helped me a lot. If I wasn't so busy I'd help you take the letters round.'

'That's all right,' said the postman. 'Any day will do for that. You don't get snow every day.' And he went off, laughing.

The next person to come in at the gate was the milk-boy. He whistled when he saw the big pile of snow and said, 'What's that going to be—a snowman?'

'A snow giant,' said Mary-Mary.

'It wants to be bigger than that, then,' said the milk-boy.

'Yes, it does,' said Mary-Mary. 'Would you like to help make it bigger?'

'What, me?' said the milk-boy. 'Oh, no, I've got work to do.'

But, all the same, he rolled up his sleeves and set to work to show Mary-Mary how to do it, and in a few minutes the snow giant reached half-way up the window. The milk-boy stepped back, puffing and blowing and wiping his face on a big red handkerchief.

'That's going to be a bit of all right,' he said. 'But I must be off.'

'Thank you very much,' said Mary-Mary. 'You *have* helped me a lot. If I wasn't so busy I'd help you with the milk-bottles.'

'That's all right,' said the milk-boy. 'Any old day will do for that.' And he ran off up the road after the milk-cart.

Mary-Mary looked at the snow giant and decided he was tall enough now. All he needed was his head. She wasn't big enough to reach up, not even if she stood on the window-sill; so she decided to make it separately and ask some one else to lift it up when it was finished.

She rolled a very big snowball to the middle of the front gate and patted it smooth. Then she put two pebbles in for eyes, a lump of snow for a nose, and a twig from the hedge to make a mouth. It began to look very jolly. Mary-Mary laughed and put her own woolly cap on top. Then she picked some small green branches from the hedge and stuck them into the snowball all round the edges of the woolly cap. They looked just like hair. Then she made some eyebrows as well, to match.

A van drew up in front of the house, and the laundry-man got down and came to the front gate with a big box under his arm. He grinned at Mary-Mary sitting in the snow by the great big snowball. Then he rested the box on the wall for a moment, and began adding up sums in a little notebook.

'I'm sorry my snow giant's head is in the way,' said Mary-Mary.

'That's all right,' said the laundry-man. 'I expect I can step over it.'

'He's got a body over there,' said Mary-Mary, pointing to it.

'That's nice,' said the laundry-man, still adding up sums.

'I think he'd really rather his head was on his body,' said Mary-Mary. 'It would be much easier for him than having it kicking around by the gate, wouldn't it?'

'Yes, I expect it would,' said the laundry-man, still busy with his notebook.

'It's so much nicer to be all in one piece, don't you think?' said Mary-Mary.

'Yes, much nicer,' said the laundry-man.

'So he'd be awfully glad if you'd do it for him,' said Mary-Mary.

The laundry-man shut his little book, put his

"I'm sorry my snow giant's head is in the way."

pencil behind his ear, and picked up the laundry box again.

'*If* you would be so kind,' said Mary-Mary very politely, and, getting up quickly, she stood in front of the snowball so that the laundry-man couldn't step over it.

'Eh?' said the man. 'What do you want me to do?'

'Put his head on for him, please,' said Mary-Mary. 'He can't do it himself and I'm not tall enough to reach.'

'Oh, I see!' said the laundry-man, laughing. 'Yes, I'll do it for you. Which way round do you want him?'

'Looking in, please,' said Mary-Mary. 'I want him to give my big brothers and sisters a very small fright, because they said they didn't believe in him.'

The laundry-man looked at the side of the snowball which had the face on it.

'Oh, yes, he's a fine fellow,' he said. 'I don't think he'll frighten them much. He's got a nice smile.'

'Yes, hasn't he?' said Mary-Mary. 'I made it. It's a twig really.'

The laundry-man lifted the snow giant's head very carefully and put it on top of the snow giant's body in front of the sitting-room window. One of the pebble eyes fell out, and some of the green hair came out from under the woolly cap; but he lifted Mary-Mary up, and she put them back in the right places.

Then Mary-Mary said, 'Thank you very much. You *have* helped me a lot. Shall I help you do the laundry to make up?'

But the laundry-man said, no, there was no need, because luckily he didn't have to wash the clothes; he only had to drive the van from house to house to collect the boxes.

When the laundry-man had driven away again, Mother made a hot chocolate drink and called all the children in from the garden.

Miriam, Martyn, Mervyn, and Meg came in, stamping the snow from their boots and blowing on their cold fingers.

'Well, how did you all get on?' said Mother.

'We haven't finished yet,' said Miriam. 'We spent such a lot of time looking for the burglar.'

'There wasn't any burglar,' said Mary-Mary.

'How do *you* know?' said the others.

'Because I know who it was,' said Mary-Mary.

'Look here—*do* you know anything about it?' said Martyn.

'Of course I do,' said Mary-Mary.

'Who was it, then?'

'I told you,' said Mary-Mary. 'It was the snow gi—'

'Oh, yes, I know all about your old snow giant,' said Martyn. 'But who was it really?'

'Me, of course,' said Mary-Mary.

'But they were huge, great footprints!' said Miriam.

'I know,' said Mary-Mary. 'I had Father's boots on. That's why I was being a snow giant, and I *did* sit down in the middle of the lawn and I *did* eat some snow.'

'*Well*, you might have told us!' said Martyn.

'Well, really,' said Mother. 'I do think you're all rather silly. Mary-Mary tried to tell you over and over again, but you just wouldn't listen.'

'Yes, but she kept on talking about a snow giant,' they said; 'and we knew there was no such thing.'

'But there *is*,' said Mary-Mary, 'and if you don't believe me go into the sitting-room and have a look.'

'Into the *sitting*-room!' said Mother. 'Oh, Mary-Mary, what *have* you been doing? Surely you haven't brought a whole lot of snow into the house! Oh, dear! Oh, dear!'

And she ran along the passage, with the others all following, and opened the door into the sitting-room. Then Mary-Mary heard Mother laughing and laughing, and she heard the others all saying, 'Oh, my goodness!' 'How did she do it?' 'Isn't it huge?' and 'I bet some one helped her!'

Then Mary-Mary began laughing too, and ran after them all. And when she saw her snow giant smiling in at the window with his twiggy mouth and his pebble eyes and his green-leaf hair sticking out from under the woolly cap she

— smiling in at the window —

laughed more than ever, because he really did look so splendid and surprising.

'Well,' said Mother, 'I think you'll all have to agree that Mary-Mary's snow giant is quite the best thing in the garden!'

And they all had to agree that he was, and Mary-Mary was so pleased with herself that she turned head over heels nine times running, all round the sitting-room floor.

'The trouble with Mary-Mary is she's much too big for her boots,' said Martyn.

'Oh, no!' said Mary-Mary, surprised. 'The boots were much too big for me.'

So there was a snow giant in Mary-Mary's garden, after all, and that is the end of the story.

THREE

Mary-Mary finds a Primrose

One day Mary-Mary had nothing special to do. So she went all round the house to see what every one else was doing.

Mother was upstairs, looking for dust-sheets. That was dull. Miriam was in the bedroom, staring at her face in the looking-glass.

'What are you looking for?' said Mary-Mary.

'Nothing,' said Miriam crossly. 'I've found it. It's a spot on my nose. Go away.'

Martyn was downstairs, looking for a piece of rope.

'What for?' said Mary-Mary.

'To practise jumping. Run away now,' he said.

Mervyn was looking for his motor-boat in the toy cupboard.

'Why?' said Mary-Mary.

'Because I want it, of course,' said Mervyn.

Meg was at the piano, staring hard at the music.

'Why don't you play a tune?' said Mary-Mary.

'Because I'm looking for the place,' said Meg. 'Go away and shut the door.'

So Mary-Mary went away and found Moppet, who was sitting on her pillow, looking over the top of the eiderdown with bright, beady black eyes.

'Every one seems to be looking for something,' said Mary-Mary to Moppet. 'We'd better go and look for something too.'

'What shall we look for?' she asked in Moppet's tiny, squeaky voice.

'Anything,' said Mary-Mary. 'It doesn't matter what. If we don't know what we're looking for we might find something really nice.'

So she carried Moppet downstairs and out into the garden. They walked all the way round the garden, but couldn't see anything special at all; so then Mary-Mary said in Moppet's voice, 'Don't let's look for anything big; let's look for something very, very small—about my size.'

'All right,' she said. And she put Moppet in her pocket and crawled along the flower-bed on her hands and knees, trying to make herself as small as Moppet.

And that was how she found the primrose.

It was growing all by itself, half hidden under dead leaves, one pretty little pale-yellow primrose.

— one pretty little pale yellow primrose —

'I do believe it's the only flower in the garden,' said Mary-Mary. 'And *I* found it! I must go and tell the others.'

She found Mother in the sitting-room, covering the tables and chairs with white dust-sheets. Mary-Mary ran in and said, 'Mother, guess what I've found!'

But Mother said, 'Not now, darling. Run away, there's a good girl. I'm busy this morning.' And she climbed up on top of a ladder and started dusting the picture-rail.

Mary-Mary crawled under a little table and began to play tents. She pulled the sheet this way and that, trying to make a nice opening for her tent, and then, because she pulled too hard, the whole table fell over on its side with a clatter and Mary-Mary was quite covered up in the dust-sheet.

Mother looked down from the top of the

ladder and said, 'Now, Mary-Mary, you really must run away. This isn't a game. This is spring cleaning.'

So Mary-Mary climbed out from under the dust-sheet and went away to tell some one else about her primrose.

She found Miriam still in the bedroom looking in the looking-glass and putting white cream on her nose.

'Miriam,' said Mary-Mary, 'shall I tell you what I've just found?'

'No,' said Miriam, 'not now. You can see I'm busy.'

Mary-Mary went up to the dressing-table and looked at the cream jar.

'That's fun,' she said. 'You look like a circus clown. I'll be a clown too.' And she put her fingers in the cream jar.

Miriam grabbed it from her. 'No, not you,' she said. 'You don't need cream on. What you need is a good wash. You're all covered in earth.'

'Why do you need it, then?' said Mary-Mary.

'Because of this spot on my nose,' said Miriam. 'Mother says it's the spring. Now, do go *away*, Mary-Mary.'

So Mary-Mary went away to find Martyn.

He had fixed up a rope in the dining-room. One end was tied to the table-leg, and the other end hung over the door-handle. Mary-Mary opened the door just as Martyn was going to jump over the rope.

'Guess what I've found, Martyn!' said Mary-Mary.

'Oh, bother!' said Martyn. 'Why must you come and interrupt me? Now, do be quiet. You can stay and watch if you like, but don't talk.'

So Mary-Mary went in and sat in the big armchair and watched Martyn. But she soon got tired of this; so she climbed up on to the back of the big chair and began jumping down into the seat every time Martyn jumped over the rope.

Suddenly there was a loud *whamm*!

'What was that?' said Mary-Mary.

'You naughty girl,' said Martyn. 'That was the spring.'

'What do you mean?' said Mary-Mary.

'The spring of the chair,' said Martyn. 'It sounds as if you've broken it by jumping on it. You'd better go away quickly before you break anything else.'

So Mary-Mary went away to find Mervyn (because she still hadn't told anybody about her primrose). Mervyn was sitting on the floor by

Whamm!

the toy cupboard with his motor-boat on his knee.

'Guess what I've found!' said Mary-Mary.

'No, not now,' said Mervyn. 'I'm busy trying to mend this.'

'What's the matter with it?' said Mary-Mary.

'I think the spring's broken,' said Mervyn.

Mary-Mary didn't want to hear any more about broken springs; so she went away to find Meg.

Meg was still playing the piano. Mary-Mary

went and stood beside her, waiting for her to finish so that she could tell her about the primrose. But Meg didn't finish. She went on and on, playing the same notes over and over again, and playing them wrong nearly every time. Mary-Mary thought it was a very loud and lumpy sort of piece, and wondered what it could be called.

Soon she grew tired of waiting for Meg to stop playing; so she began playing herself, very softly, on the low notes.

'Stop it,' said Meg, still playing hard.

So Mary-Mary went round to the other side and began playing very softly on the high notes.

'Go *away*,' said Meg, and stopped playing.

'Would you like to hear what I've found?' said Mary-Mary.

'No, I wouldn't,' said Meg. 'Can't you see I'm practising?'

'What are you practising for?' said Mary-Mary.

'For the school concert,' said Meg. 'And it's jolly hard.'

'It sounds it,' said Mary-Mary. 'Is it about a giant? Or is it elephants playing ball?'

'Don't be silly,' said Meg. 'It's called Spring Song. Now do go *away* and stop bothering.'

So Mary-Mary did go away; and, because

there was no one else to tell about the primrose, she went out of the front door and down the front path, and started swinging on the front gate. It was warm and sunny, and some birds in the tree close by were chirping and twittering loudly.

Mr Bassett came along the road, whistling to himself. He smiled when he saw Mary-Mary, and said, 'Hallo.'

'Hallo,' said Mary-Mary. 'Why are you whistling?'

'Because it's such a lovely day,' said Mr Bassett. 'Spring is coming, Mary-Mary.'

'I know,' said Mary-Mary. 'It's come already in our house.'

'How do you mean?' said Mr Bassett.

'Well,' said Mary-Mary. 'Mother's spring-cleaning, and Miriam's got a spot on her nose (and she says that's the spring), and I jumped on a chair and it made a funny noise (and Martyn said *that* was the spring, too), and Mervyn's putting a new spring in his motor-boat, and Meg's playing a piece like elephants dancing on the piano (and she said *that* was a Spring Song), so I think we've got a lot more spring than we need in our house.'

'Oh, dear,' said Mr Bassett, 'I didn't mean spring-cleaning and things like that. I was thinking about the birds all nesting in the trees, and the ice being melted on the pond, and the spring flowers that will soon be coming up in the garden.'

Then Mary-Mary said, 'Guess what I've found!'

And Mr Bassett said, 'A crocus?'

And Mary-Mary said, 'No. A primrose.'

And Mr Bassett said, 'Well, that really *is* a bit of spring! They must all be coming up in Bramley Woods too.'

'The others are all too busy to come and see my primrose,' said Mary-Mary; 'so they don't know about it yet.'

'Then you'll have to take it to them,' said Mr Bassett.

So Mary-Mary went and picked her primrose, and, as she hadn't got a vase, she put it in a jam-jar filled with water. Then, when it was dinner-time, while Mother was fetching the plates in from the kitchen, Mary-Mary put the primrose in the jar on the table in front of Mother's place.

'Whatever's that?' said Miriam.

'One flower,' said Martyn.

'In a great big jam-jar,' said Mervyn.

'It looks silly all by itself,' said Meg.

Then they all said together, 'Don't put it

there, Mary-Mary.' 'Mother won't have room to put the plates down.' 'You're spilling the water on the cloth.' 'The jar's too big for it.'

Then Mary-Mary suddenly began shouting out in a loud, cross voice, 'I think you're all jolly silly. If you weren't so cross and busy and

" I think you're all jolly silly "

beastly, bothering about spring-cleaning and spring spots and broken chair-springs and motor-boat springs and lumpy old Spring Songs on the piano you might have found this primrose yourselves, and *then* you might have remembered that it was really spring—'

Just then Mother came in with the plates, and when she saw the primrose in the jam-jar she said, 'Oh, it's a lovely little primrose! The first I've seen this year. Who found it?'

But Mary-Mary was still talking to the others (though she wasn't shouting quite so loudly now) '—and if one primrose can grow in our garden,' she said, 'when every one's cross and busy and beastly and not bothering about it at all, then there must be hundreds and *hundreds* of primroses growing in Bramley Woods where nobody's cross and busy and beastly. And if *I* were a mother with a whole lot of cross and busy and beastly children I'd go to Bramley Woods and have a picnic there and pick primroses!'

Then Miriam and Martyn and Mervyn and Meg all started talking at once. But Mother said, 'No, hush. Mary-Mary is quite right. I think we really had forgotten it was spring, and I'd quite forgotten about the primroses in Bramley Woods. They must be lovely there just now. Shall we do as Mary-Mary says and all have a picnic?'

Then every one said, 'Oh, yes!' 'Hooray!' 'A picnic!' 'How clever of Mary-Mary to have thought of it!'

And Mother said, 'Yes, it shall be Mary-

Mary's own picnic, because she is the only person who remembered it was really spring!'

So they all went for a picnic to Bramley Woods because Mary-Mary had found the very first primrose, and that is the end of the story.

FOUR

Mary-Mary and Miss Muffin

One day Mary-Mary was bored. All her big brothers and sisters were reading or writing or drawing or knitting, but Mary-Mary was doing nothing.

She tried talking to them, she tried jumping up and down in front of them, she tried making faces at them; but all they said was, 'Oh, stop bothering, Mary-Mary!'

So Mary-Mary stopped bothering. Instead, she said in a dreamy voice, 'I think it's time Miss Muffin came again.'

When Mary-Mary said this everybody groaned, because they knew what it meant.

It meant that Mary-Mary, dressed in some of Mother's old clothes, was going to come knocking at the front door, saying she was Miss Muffin and had come to tea. Then every one had to be polite to her and ask her in and treat her as if she were a real visitor. If they didn't Miss Muffin made such a scene, marching up and down in front of the gate and shouting that 'some people had no manners,' that they were all ashamed of her and had to hurry out and bring her indoors before a crowd collected.

The first time Mary-Mary had come knocking on the door, saying she was Miss Muffin, it had been a great success. Father had been at home, and he had invited her in most politely and never shown that he guessed it might really be Mary-Mary. And when the others had started to say, 'Don't be silly—we know who you are really,' Father had looked quite shocked and said, 'Hush! It's all right for you to be rude to each other or to Mary-Mary; but Miss Muffin is a visitor and must be treated politely.'

Mary-Mary had loved this, of course, and Miriam, Martyn, Mervyn, and Meg were afraid she would want to be Miss Muffin every day, But Father had said, quite definitely, as he was showing her out of the door, 'Good-bye, Miss Muffin. It *has* been nice having you. We shall look forward to your coming again, *but that won't be for a long while, of course.*'

Mary-Mary had started to say, 'Oh, but I could come again to-morrow . . .'

But Father had put his finger on his lips and said, 'No—not if you are really Miss Muffin, because Miss Muffin is a lady, and ladies know that they can't come to tea very often without being invited.'

"I think it's time Miss Muffin came again."

'Yes, of course,' said Mary-Mary in Miss Muffin's voice. 'I shall only come very sometimes, not at all very often. Thank you for such a nice afternoon. Your children have been most polite to me.'

For a while Mary-Mary had been quite good about only being Miss Muffin sometimes and not very often. But soon she took to being Miss Muffin oftener and oftener, and once Miss Muffin had even invited herself to tea two days running. Miriam, Martyn, Mervyn, and Meg had shut the door in her face, and it was then that Miss Muffin had made the dreadful scene outside the front gate.

So to-day, when Mary-Mary said, 'I think it's time Miss Muffin came again,' everybody groaned.

Then Mother said quickly, 'No, I can't do with any visitors to-day—I'm too busy. Miss Muffin must come another day.'

'When?' said Mary-Mary. 'To-morrow?'

'Perhaps,' said Mother. 'It all depends how busy I am. No, not to-morrow. It's the Garden Fête. I must bake some cakes to take along there.'

The Garden Fête was going to be held two afternoons running at the house of a lady called Miss Stokes. She had a large garden, and if the weather was fine the stalls and the teas were going to be out of doors.

'Can we go to the Garden Fête too?' said Miriam.

'Yes,' said Mother. 'We will all go to-morrow.'

'Oh, *why* not to-day?' said Miriam, Martyn, Mervyn, and Meg all together.

'I told you why,' said Mother. 'But now I

come to think of it, there's really no reason why you shouldn't go by yourselves.'

Miriam, Martyn, Mervyn, and Meg were all very pleased.

'But do we have to take Mary-Mary?' they said.

'No. You four go on your own to-day,' said Mother. 'I'll take Mary-Mary to-morrow.'

Then she gave them threepence each to get in (because it was half-price for children) and ninepence each to spend there.

Mary-Mary stood at the gate and watched them go. They felt rather sorry for her when they saw her standing there.

'Never mind,' they said. 'Perhaps Miss Muffin can come another day.'

'Yes, perhaps she can,' said Mary-Mary, 'and perhaps she can't. And perhaps she can come to-day and perhaps she can't. It all depends how busy she is.'

They looked rather surprised at this. Then Miriam said, 'Come on, she's only pretending. Let's go.' And they all said, 'Never mind, Mary-Mary,' again, and waved good-bye to her all the way down the road.

Mary-Mary went on thinking rather hard about Miss Muffin.

'Perhaps she can and perhaps she can't,'

she said out loud, to nobody in particular.
'It all depends how busy she is. I'd better find
out.'

Then she dialled a pretend telephone number
on the gate, pulled a branch of the hedge close
to her ear, and said very fast, in an important,
grown-up voice, '*Ting-a-ling, ting-a-ling*. Hallo,
Miss Muffin—is that you? Are you busy to-day?
No, I'm bored to death. Oh, good. Well, there's
a Garden Fête at Miss Stokes' house. Oh,
hooray—thank you for telling me. I could just
do with a Garden Fête. I've never been to one
before. No, I thought you hadn't. Good-bye.'

'Well, that settles that,' said Mary-Mary.
'Miss Muffin *is* coming to-day. I *thought* she
was.'

She ran quickly upstairs, pulled out a box
from under her bed, and took out Miss Muffin's
old, battered hat and purple-flowered dress.
Then she ran downstairs again and put them
on in front of the hall mirror, nodding at herself
and talking to herself all the time.

In the kitchen she could hear Mother getting
out the baking-tins, then some one knocking at
the back door, then Mrs Merry's voice saying
she'd just popped in as she was passing.

'That's lucky,' said Mary-Mary, putting on
the old, battered hat. 'Mrs Merry's just popped

in, so I'll just pop out. When Mrs Merry pops in she doesn't pop out again for ages and ages; so if I pop out now no one'll miss me. But just in *case* they do, I'll pop a note in the letter-box saying I've popped out; then I'll pop off.'

'That sounded rather good,' said Mary-Mary. 'I wish I could remember how I did it.'

Then she wrote a note saying, 'Dear Mrs Madam, Just popped out to the Fête. Yours truly, Miss Muffin,' and popped it in the letter-box.

Last of all she ran out and dug up her dreadful old handbag out of the sandpit. She had to keep it there when she wasn't using it because it was so very old and dreadful-looking that people always wanted to throw it away when they saw it lying around. It had belonged to Mother a very long while ago.

She opened it to see what was inside. There were only two buttons, an elastic band, and an empty cigarette packet.

'Never mind,' said Miss Muffin. 'Money isn't everything.' And she closed it with a snap and set off to the Garden Fête.

She ran all the way there, holding up her skirt so as not to trip over it. On the fence outside Miss Stokes' house was a large notice which she stopped to read. It said:

COME TO THE GARDEN FÊTE
STALLS, SIDESHOWS, AND STRAWBERRY
TEAS
PLEASE WALK IN

'Thank you, I will,' said Miss Muffin, and she straightened her hat and walked in.

At the top of the drive a lady was sitting at a little table taking money from the people who were coming in (sixpence for grown-ups and half-price for children). Miss Muffin bent down

—a large notice which she stopped to read

"Who was that funny little person?"

low, picked up her skirt, and ran as fast as she could right past the little table and through a rose arch into the garden. The lady at the table looked up quickly.

'Who was that funny little person?' she said.

But nobody seemed to know.

'Oh, well, I expect she was something to do with one of the sideshows,' said the lady, and went on taking the sixpences.

Miriam, Martyn, Mervyn, and Meg each spent their ninepence at the Garden Fête. First they spent threepence each on an ice-cream (but that didn't last long). Then they spent threepence each on the hoop-la stall (but none of them won anything). Then they spent three-pence each on the lucky dip.

Miriam won two marbles.

'What ever do I want with those?' she said.

Martyn won a doll's knife and fork.

'That's no use to me,' he said.

Mervyn won a pink plastic hair-slide, but didn't even feel funny enough to put it on. And Meg won a box of pistol caps.

'I should call that an unlucky dip,' said Martyn. 'I'd rather have had another ice-cream.'

'So would I,' said the others. Then they all said together. 'Never mind –we'll save them for Mary-Mary.'

After that they stood in a group near the tea garden, sadly watching the people having strawberry teas at the little tables and wishing they had saved their ice-creams till now instead of buying them right at the beginning.

Just as they were wondering whether to go home the four Merry children came by. Barbara, Billy, Bunty, and Bob were all laughing and looking very jolly.

'I say!' said Barbara to Miriam. 'Have you seen who's at the White Elephant stall?'

'The *what*?' said Miriam. 'Surely they haven't got elephants here?'

'No, of course not. "White elephants" just means anything you don't want and don't know how to get rid of. People bring them to fêtes, and then sometimes other people buy them.' She began laughing again; so did the others.

'Well, what's so funny about that?' said Miriam, who was beginning to want her tea quite a lot.

'It isn't funny at all,' said Martyn, who was hungry.

'I don't see anything to laugh at,' said Mervyn, who was thirsty.

'Nor do I,' said Meg, who was tired.

'You will if you go to the White Elephant stall,' said the Merrys, and they all went off, laughing.

Just then Miss Stokes came hurrying out of the tea garden.

'Hallo! How are you all?' she said. 'And how is your dear mother? I haven't seen her for such a long time. And how is your baby brother, or is it a sister?'

'We have a little sister,' said Miriam.

'But she's not quite a baby any more,' said Martyn.

'She's at home with Mother,' said Mervyn.

'They're coming to-morrow,' said Meg.

'Well, that *is* nice,' said Miss Stokes. 'I shall look forward to seeing them both. And now you must come and see my stall—it's the White Elephant stall and I've been doing so well. I've got a wonderful helper.'

She led them down to the far end of the garden, where they saw quite a little crowd collected round one of the stalls. As they came nearer they heard people laughing. Then all of a sudden Martyn said, 'Look who's there!'

They all looked, and high up above the people's heads, standing on the stall itself, what should they see but a funny little person, no bigger than Mary-Mary, in a battered old hat and a purple-flowered dress.

'Why, it's Mm—!' Miriam was just going to say 'Mary-Mary,' but Miss Stokes said, 'Miss Muffin, that's right. It's little Miss Muffin. Do you know her?'

'Well, sort of,' mumbled Miriam, Martyn, Mervyn, and Meg. 'We have seen her before.'

'That's nice,' said Miss Stokes; 'then you must come and meet her. She's been *such* a success. I've sold nearly everything off my stall since she started helping me. Such a funny little thing—she told me her name was Muffin, but I don't know any family of that name. I was a bit worried at first —she seemed so small to be here alone; but she said she'd just popped in as she was passing, and she had some big brothers and sisters here. So I supposed it was all right, and she's been *such* a success on the stall.'

Miss Stokes pushed her way through the crowd with the others following. It was quite difficult to get near the stall, because so many people were coming away with their arms full of things: old lampshades, picture-frames, china ornaments, and all sorts of odds and ends. One man was even wheeling an old pram full of odd-sized dinner plates, old hats, and saucepans.

'Yes,' said Miss Stokes in a whisper, 'they've all been bought at the White Elephant stall!'

They pushed their way nearer and saw that Miss Muffin, on top of the stall, was waving a large bunch of paper flowers.

'Only threepence!' she was calling out in a high, squeaky voice. 'Who'll buy a big bunch of flowers for threepence?'

'What should I do with those?' said a man in the front.

'You could put one in your buttonhole, and give the rest to your lady,' said Miss Muffin. 'And here's a jug, a very nice jug. Who'd like to buy this jug?' She picked up a large white bedroom jug that was standing in a basin beside her.

'What's it for?' said the man down in front.

Miss Muffin looked at it. 'Well, it's a bit big for milk,' she said, 'but you could use it for a vase. The handle makes it easier to fill.' She put the bunch of paper flowers in it. 'There you are,' she said, 'if you buy both together they're very pretty.'

'But what about the basin?' said the man.

'Oh, that's for sailing boats in, if you're a man, or making puddings in, if you're a lady. It's a very useful basin—you can use it for both.'

'But I haven't got a boat,' said the man, smiling, 'and my lady has a pudding basin already. What should I do with it?'

Miss Muffin thought hard, then she said brightly, 'I know—you could wash in it!'

Every one laughed because that was what the basin was really for; then the man said, 'All right, you win,' and he handed up the money for all three.

He took one of the paper flowers and put it in his buttonhole, then he handed the rest of the bunch back to Miss Muffin.

'Keep those for yourself,' he said. Then off he went, carrying the big china jug and basin.

'Oh, goody!' said Miss Stokes. 'I never thought we'd get rid of those.' Then she pushed her way to the front.

"What should I do with those?" said a man in the front —

'Miss Muffin,' she called, 'here are some friends of yours. Would you like to come down now and see them? You've done so well I've hardly anything left to sell; so if you'd like to take your friends to tea I'll give you the tickets.'

So Miss Muffin was lifted down from the stall, and Miss Stokes thanked her very much indeed for her valuable help, and brought out a long strip of pink paper, which was five tea tickets all joined together.

'Take those to the tea garden,' she said, 'and you and your friends will just be in nice time for the strawberry teas.'

So Miriam, Martyn, Mervyn, and Meg all sat at a table under a large striped umbrella with Miss Muffin, and had strawberries and bread and butter and jam, and little iced cakes as well.

'You see,' said Mary-Mary, nodding at them under the large battered hat and wiping her sticky fingers on the purple-flowered dress, 'Miss Muffin is quite a useful person to know sometimes. You ought to be polite to her *every* time she comes.'

So Mary-Mary and her big brothers and sisters all had strawberry teas at the Garden Fête, thanks to Miss Muffin, and that is the end of the story.

FIVE

Mary-Mary makes the Morning Exciting

One Saturday morning Mary-Mary's mother was out, and Mary-Mary's big brothers and sisters were all feeling rather dull. They wandered about the house and in and out of the garden, saying, 'What shall we do? How *boring* everything is! I wish something interesting would happen.'

'What sort of interesting?' said Mary-Mary, who was blowing air into a paper bag.

'Oh, anything,' said Miriam.

'Some men coming to dig up the road,' said Martyn.

'Or the fire engine coming,' said Mervyn.

'Or some one cutting a tree down,' said Meg.

Mary-Mary screwed up the top of the bag, then clapped her hands on it so that it burst with a loud pop. Then she said, 'If *I* wanted something interesting to happen I'd make it happen,' and she stumped off upstairs.

A few minutes later Miriam, Martyn, Mervyn and Meg heard a great thumping and bumping noise going on overhead. They all ran out into the hall and shouted up the stairs, 'What ever are you doing, Mary-Mary?'

'Something exciting,' said Mary-Mary.

'Well, stop it,' they said.

'You won't say that when you see me come floating down the stairs,' said Mary-Mary.

'What ever do you mean?' said Miriam.

'I'm learning to fly,' said Mary-Mary.

'It sounds as if you're jumping off the bed,' said Miriam.

'Oh, no, I'm *flying* off the bed,' said Mary-Mary. 'Like Peter Pan.'

'Well, don't,' said Miriam. 'The ceiling will fall down.'

'Well, that would be exciting too,' said Mary-Mary.

'Don't be silly,' said Miriam, Martyn, Mervyn, and Meg all together, and they went back into the sitting-room.

Mary-Mary stopped trying to fly, and instead she fetched Moppet from the top of the toy cupboard and whispered in his ear, 'You and I will go and do something exciting all by ourselves. We'll play shipwrecks in the bath.'

She fetched her little sailing-boat and carried it into the bathroom with Moppet. Then she filled the bath with water, put Moppet in the little boat, and floated him out to sea in the middle of the bath.

Moppet floated round quite nicely in the little boat for a while, then Mary-Mary said, 'Look out, sailor—there's a storm coming up in a minute!' And she took the bath-brush and stirred up the water into little waves, so that the boat rocked up and down, just as if it were in a rough sea.

Some of the water splashed over the edge of the bath and made Mary-Mary's feet wet, so she took off her shoes and socks. Then she locked the bathroom door.

'I will hide the key in a safe and secret place,' she said to Moppet, 'because it would be a pity if some one came in while the sea was rough and interrupted me just as I was going to save you.'

Then, when she had hidden the key, she stirred up some more waves with the bath-brush, and slowly the little boat filled with water and began to sink.

'Save me!' she squeaked in Moppet's voice.

'Yes,' said Mary-Mary in a beautiful, dreamy voice. 'I am a mermaid and I will save you.'

She reached down into the water and pulled Moppet out just before the little boat sank to the bottom. Then she sat on the edge of the bath, at the tap end, with Moppet in her lap.

'Oh, thank you, thank you!' she squeaked.
'You saved my life. Tell me who you are.'

'I am a mermaid,' sang Mary-Mary in the
beautiful dreamy voice, 'and I am sitting on a
rock in the middle of the sea, combing my
beautiful long hair.' And, as she had no comb,
she brushed her hair with the big bath-brush
until it stood out in short, wet spikes all round
her head.

'I have a beautiful palace at the bottom of the
sea, all made of shells,' she sang, 'and you shall
come there with me and be my mermouse, and
we will live happily ever after.'

Then she let the plug out, and when the water
had run away she and Moppet climbed in and
sat in the bottom of the bath and had a large
pretend feast of fish and shrimps in the mermaid's palace.

But the bottom of the bath was cold and wet.
So after a while Mary-Mary said to Moppet,
'I'm getting rather tired of living happily ever
after, aren't you? Let's get out and be ordinary
people again.' And they climbed out of the bath
and went to open the door. But the door of the
bathroom was locked.

Mary-Mary rattled the handle; then she remembered.

'Of course,' she said. 'I locked it myself. And I

" – in the middle of the sea, combing my beautiful long hair – "

hid the key in a safe and secret place. Now, I wonder where that could have been? Oh, yes— I expect it was under the bath.'

But it wasn't. Mary-Mary looked all round the bathroom, under the bath, in the laundry box, and on the window-sill; but she couldn't find the key anywhere.

'It *must* have been a safe and secret place if I can't even find it myself,' she said.

Then she heard the others calling to her. 'Where are you, Mary-Mary?'

—but she couldn't find the key anywhere—

'I'm here,' said Mary-Mary.

'Come down at once,' said Miriam.

'I can't,' said Mary-Mary.

'Why not?' said Martyn.

'I can't unlock the door,' said Mary-Mary.

'Oh, goodness!' said Meg. 'Now what are we going to do?'

They all stood outside the door and rattled the handle and talked and shouted and banged on the door, but still Mary-Mary was shut up inside.

'Can't you really remember where you put the key?' said Miriam.

'No, truly I can't,' said Mary-Mary. And she truly couldn't. 'Perhaps it's gone down the plug-hole,' she said.

'Oh, you silly girl,' said Miriam, Martyn, Mervyn, and Meg all together, and they all went on talking and arguing about how they should get her out.

Miriam went to ask Miss Summers next door if she could help, but Miss Summers was out. Then Meg went to ask Mr Bassett, who lived near by; but he was out too.

Mary-Mary began to get tired of being shut up in the bathroom.

'I'm getting hungry,' she said.

'Oh, goodness!' said Meg, outside the door. 'Will she starve?'

'Of course she won't,' said Mervyn.

'But we ought to get her out, all the same,' said Martyn.

'What ever shall we do?' said Miriam.

They whispered and talked outside the door for a bit longer. Then all of a sudden Martyn said, 'I know! We could get the fire brigade.'

'But why?' said the others. 'There isn't a fire.'

'No,' said Martyn, 'but they have long ladders and things. I believe that's what people do when they get stuck in places: they ask the firemen to come and get them out.'

'Yes, of course,' said Miriam. 'Why didn't I think of it before? We'd better go and telephone them.'

Then Mary-Mary heard them all running away downstairs.

She forgot to feel hungry any more and began to feel rather excited, looking forward to the firemen coming. But what a pity it would be, she thought, if she should miss seeing the fire engine drive up to the house.

'If only I could find the key I could get out and watch them arrive,' she said to herself. 'Anyway, I may as well get all ready just in case I find it.'

So she tidied up the bathroom and put on her socks, and then, when she went to put on her shoe, out fell the key on to the floor!

'Of course!' said Mary-Mary. 'Now I remember. I put it in my shoe on purpose so that I could forget where it was if anyone came up suddenly and told me to open the door.'

When Miriam, Martyn, Mervyn, and Meg had finished telephoning they all went on to the front step to wait for the fire brigade.

In a very short while they heard the clanging of a bell, and a moment later the big red fire engine came roaring up the road and stopped at

— the big red fire engine —

the front gate. Then four firemen, in helmets and big black boots, jumped quickly down and ran one after the other up the front path to the house. It was a splendid sight.

Miriam explained all about how her poor little sister had been locked up in the bathroom for hours, and Mother was out, and they hadn't known what to do.

'That's all right,' said the biggest fireman. 'Don't you worry. We'll have her out in no time.'

Then the four firemen went tramping up the stairs in their big black boots, with Miriam,

Martyn, Mervyn, and Meg all following behind and telling them which way to go.

But when they got to the landing they all stopped and stared at each other, and the four children said, 'Oh!' and the four firemen said, 'What's the meaning of this? Have you children been playing a joke on us?' For the bathroom door was wide open and there was no Mary-Mary to be seen!

'No, truly she was here!' they cried. 'She was locked in, and we didn't know what to do. Oh, where can she be?' And they all ran from room to room calling her.

Then one of the firemen opened the front bedroom window, and they all looked down into the garden, and there what should they see but Mary-Mary standing by the gate with a whole crowd of people.

The four Merry children were there, and Tommy from up the road, and Stanley, the grocer's boy, with his bicycle, and quite a few grown-ups as well. And Mary-Mary was waving her hand at the fire engine, just as if she owned it, and saying, 'Yes, it is nice, isn't it? It was ordered specially for me on the telephone.'

'But where's the fire?' said Stanley, the grocer's boy.

'There isn't one,' said Mary-Mary. 'Don't be

" It was ordered specially for me "

silly. We didn't want a fire; we only wanted a
fire engine.'

'Ooh, you are lucky!' said Tommy from up
the road. 'I wish the fire engine would come to
our house.'

Just then Miriam and the others saw Mother
hurrying up the road with her shopping-basket
on her arm. They all ran downstairs as fast as
they could to meet her.

'It's all right,' they cried, 'there isn't a fire!'
Then they told her all about what had hap-
pened.

'Thank goodness for that!' said Mother, and
she hurried indoors and told the firemen how

sorry she was, and how the children had really thought they were doing the right thing. Then she made them all a cup of tea.

The firemen were very nice and said accidents did happen sometimes, and they were glad the children hadn't been playing a joke on them, because that would be a very serious matter. Then every one suddenly remembered that Mary-Mary was still outside the front gate. So Mother sent Miriam to fetch her in.

Mary-Mary came in with her wet hair still sticking out in spikes all round her head, and her hands and knees black where she had climbed up on the wall to watch the fire engine arrive. Her face was black too, where she had rubbed it with her hands.

'I *know* now what I'm going to be when I grow up,' she said, smiling brightly at them all. 'I'm going to be a fire lady.'

'So you're the young lady who was locked up in the coal cellar?' said one of the firemen.

'Oh, no,' said Mary-Mary. 'I was locked up in the bathroom.'

'Were you really, now?' said the fireman. 'I wonder what made me think it was the coal cellar.'

Mary-Mary couldn't think either; but, as everybody laughed, she laughed too. It was fun having four real firemen drinking tea in her house on a Saturday morning.

When they had finished their tea the firemen showed Miriam, Martyn, Mervyn, and Meg all sorts of interesting things: the ladders with hooks on them for climbing up the walls of houses; the hoses, coiled up tightly like Swiss rolls, that could be joined together to make one long one if they wanted it; and even the little iron lid that covered the hole in the road where they got the water to put out a fire.

Then they all said good-bye, and thank you for the tea, and thank you for coming; and Miriam, Martyn, Mervyn, Meg and Mary-Mary waved until the fire engine was out of sight.

'Well, that *was* fun!' said Miriam.

'Just what we wanted!' said Martyn.

'Better than having the road dug up,' said Mervyn.

'Or a tree cut down,' said Meg.

'I'm so glad you liked it,' said Mary-Mary, smiling proudly at them all.

'Good gracious, Mary-Mary!' they said. 'Do you mean to say you did all that on purpose?'

'No, not quite,' said Mary-Mary. 'I really did lose the key. But when I found it again I thought how disappointed you'd all be, because

I knew you so specially wanted something interesting to happen. And I couldn't dig up the road for you, or cut a tree down, but I'd jolly nearly got you a fire engine without meaning to, so I ran away and hid because I thought it would be such a pity to spoil it.'

'That *was* sweet of you,' said Miriam.

'You *are* a sport,' said Martyn.

'Thanks *awfully*, Mary-Mary,' said Mervyn.

'But you'd better not do it again,' said Meg.

'Oh, no,' said Mary-Mary, 'once is enough. But I am glad you all enjoyed it.'

So Mary-Mary made the morning exciting, after all, and that is the end of the story.

Mary-Mary

JOAN G. ROBINSON

Mary-Mary is the youngest in her family, but she manages *quite* well all the same. It's Mary-Mary who gets herself invited out to tea as a 'proper visitor', wearing her best net curtain!

Mary-Mary runs away from home, but she only goes as far as nice Mr Bassett's. He has rabbits to feed and ludo to play. Before long her brothers and sisters *ask* her to come home, please.

Lots of good things happen to Mary-Mary – and she makes sure they do!

More Mary-Mary is also an Armada Lion.

More About Paddington

MICHAEL BOND

'Bears like Paddington are very rare,' says Mrs Bird, 'and a good thing too, or it would cost us a small fortune in marmalade.'

It's a good thing for *lots* of reasons that bears like Paddington are rare. His adventures are far from ordinary. And as he says himself, 'Things happen to me – I'm that sort of bear.' With his attempts at home decorating, detective work and photography the Brown family soon find that Paddington causes his own particular brand of chaos.

More About Paddington is the second of Michael Bond's books about Paddington. It is best read after *A Bear Called Paddington* which is also an Armada Lion. Both books will particularly appeal to children up to the age of eight.